THE CHRISTMAS COOKIE SPRINKLE SNITCHER

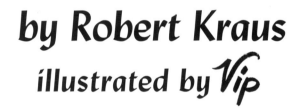

by Robert Kraus

illustrated by Vip

Purple House Press

Kentucky

TO
THE QUIET WOMAN

Published by Purple House Press, PO Box 787, Cynthiana, KY, 41031

All rights reserved.
Text copyright © 1969 Windmill Books, Inc.
Illustrations copyright © 1969 by Virgil Partch
Copyright renewed © 1997 by Peter Partch, Anna Partch-Couch and Nick Partch
Published by arrangement with Simon & Schuster Children's Publishing Division.

ISBN 978-1-930900-44-8   LCCN 2009941548

Your favorite childhood books are back!
Read about more Classic Books for Children at
purplehousepress.com

Printed in South Korea by PACOM
6 7 8 9 10

In a neat little village
all covered with snow,
sleep apple-cheeked children
their hearts all aglow,
dreaming of morning, when they will awake,
hungry for cookies their mothers will bake.

But…
high in the sky,
while children all dream,
The
Christmas
Cookie
Sprinkle
Snitcher
flies, teeth all agleam!

He lands with a bump,
then quick as a wink,
he's into the pantry
snitching a sprink!
With a toss of his head
and a lick of his chops,
into his mouth
cookie sprinkles he pops.

All the rest of the sprinks
he pours into his sack,
then tosses his sprinkle sack
onto his back.
Each villager's house
he de-sprinkles with glee.
"The more sprinkles I snitch
the more sprinkles for me!"
His sack is soon bulging
with sprinkles galore,
so his pockets he fills,
then de-sprinkles the store!

At midnight's last stroke
the village is bare —
Not one unsnitched sprinkle
is there anywhere!
Happy at last
that he's snitched all the sprinks,
the Snitcher flies home

to snatch forty winks.

Next morning at dawn, all the children awake,
eager for cookies their mothers will bake.
The mothers sing carols and roll out the dough,
cutting out cookies row upon row.

Cookie reindeer, cookie stars, cookie Santas, cookie cars.
Cookies round, cookies square, Christmas cookies everywhere.
Cookies placed in baking trays to celebrate the holidays.

Then the mothers reach for sprinkles!
Every mother's cupboard's bare!
Not one single solitary
cookie sprinkle anywhere!

And…
Christmas cookies without sprinkles
are like raisins without wrinkles,
and like sleigh bells without tinkles
are Christmas cookies without sprinkles.

All the children start to cry.
Not one child has one dry eye.
Moms start crying.
So do Pops.
Granny telephones the cops!

The Chief of Police
says with a sob,
"The Christmas Cookie Sprinkle Snitcher's
pulled this job!
He's got super powers—
He's some sort of mystic—
I'll never catch him—
Let's be realistic!"

But a plucky kid named Little Nat
knew in a flash that he had to act fast,
or Christmas cookie baking time
soon would be past.
Nat dried both his eyes
and bundled up tight.
"I'll bring back the sprinkles,"
he vowed, "before night."

Though the Snitcher was gone,
he'd left a trail
of dropped cookie sprinkles.
Nat said, "I'll not fail.
The trail of snitched sprinkles
on this cobblestone street
will lead me, I'm sure,
to the Snitcher's retreat."

Through back yards and alleys piled high with debris,
the sprinkle trail wound on and on endlessly.

Through snow-covered woods...
on ice floes in rivers...

Poor Nat got the shakes...
Poor Nat got the shivers...

Nat's knees were cold, Nat's feet were sore,
but he made it on courage to the Snitcher's front door.
At the door Nat did rap. At the door Nat did tap.

But inside the Snitcher was snatching a nap.
Nat kept rapping, Nat kept tapping.
The Sprinkle Snitcher just kept napping.

The Snitcher at last awoke with a snore,
leaped to his feet and flung open the door!
Nat fell on his face.

The Snitcher said, "Pardon the looks of the place.
I've been out snitching sprinkles. It's my Christmas fun.
And that's why my housecleaning hasn't been done."

"Your Christmas fun, Snitcher," Little Nat said,
"Has driven the whole village out of its head!
For Christmas cookies without sprinkles
are like raisins without wrinkles,
and like sleigh bells without tinkles
are Christmas cookies without sprinkles."
"I didn't mean to spoil
no one's Christmas fun.
I'm ashamed," sobbed the Snitcher,
"Ashamed what I done."

"Don't cry, Snitch," said Nat.
"There's no time to moan,
and please may I use
your telephone?"
"Sure," sobbed the Snitcher,
"You certainly can."
So Nat called his mother
and outlined his plan.
"Now dry your eyes, Snitcher,"
Little Nat said.
"Pack up your sprinkles,
our work lies ahead!"

Out through the door,
and into the air,
back to the village,
flew the curious pair.

As they circled on high
Nat looked below
and saw all the villagers,
faces aglow.

Each village woman, child and man,
with unsprinkled cookies
unbaked in a pan.
Then sprinkles swirled down
like new-fallen snow
making beautiful patterns
on cookies below.

And...

Christmas cookies all had sprinkles
just like raisins all had wrinkles
and like sleigh bells all had tinkles
Christmas cookies all had sprinkles.

"You've taught me a lesson,
Little Nat," said the Snitcher.
"Though I haven't a sprinkle
I've never been richer.
I know now that Christmas
is not being greedy.

Christmas is spreading
sprinks to the needy!"